Lulu
and the Cat in the Bag

Look out for more books by

Hilary McKay

Lulu and the Duck in the Park

Lulu and the Dog from the Sea

Charlie and the Cat Flap

Charlie and the Great Escape

Charlie and the Big Snow

Charlie and the Rocket Boy

Charlie and the Cheese and Onion Crisps

Charlie and the Haunted Tent

Charlie and the Tooth Fairy

Charlie and the Big Birthday Bash

www.hilarymckay.co.uk

Lulu
and the Cat in the Bag

Hilary McKay

Illustrated by Priscilla Lamont

SCHOLASTIC

First published in the UK in 2011 by Scholastic Children's Books
An imprint of Scholastic Ltd
Euston House, 24 Eversholt Street
London, NW1 1DB, UK
Registered office: Westfield Road, Southam, Warwickshire, CV47 0RA
SCHOLASTIC and associated logos are trademarks and/or
registered trademarks of Scholastic Inc.

Text copyright © Hilary McKay, 2011
Illustrations copyright © Priscilla Lamont 2011

The rights of Hilary McKay and Priscilla Lamont to be identified as the
author and illustrator of this work have been asserted by them.

Cover illustration © Priscilla Lamont 2011

ISBN 978 1 407 11790 4

by ... ot,
in ar ... circulated
No p ... published.
o ... val system,
... hanical,
... ritten

Papers used by Scholastic Children's Books are made from
wood grown in sustainable forests.

1 3 5 7 9 10 8 6 4 2

www.scholastic.co.uk/zone

Chapter One

The Cat in the Bag

The bag on the doorstep was enormous.

Tied at the top, like a giant shoe bag.

Heavy and lumpy, as if it were
filled with potatoes.

Warm as sunshine, and. . .

"Snoring!" said Lulu,
bending close to listen.
"It's something alive!"

"Alive?" asked
Lulu's cousin
Mellie,

who was staying at Lulu's house, and she stepped hurriedly backwards.

Mellie was a thinker. She could think of lots of alive things that might be in that bag that should not be let out.

"Alive?" repeated Mellie. "Don't just open it then, Lulu! Work out what it is first!"

But Lulu was already struggling to undo the hard knot of cord that tied the bag. She tugged with her fingers, and when that did not work she tugged with her teeth. She was doing this when she was grabbed from behind by Nan.

Nan was the grandmother of Lulu and Mellie. She also was staying at Lulu's house. She was taking care of the girls while their parents were away. Mellie's mother had won a competition. The prize was a holiday, a week in a hotel in a Spanish city. Lulu's parents had gone as well.

Lulu and Mellie could have gone too, but "*A week in a city?*" Mellie had wailed. A morning at the shops was almost more than Mellie could bear.

Lulu had not been pleased either. "A hotel?" she had asked. "The dogs won't like that!"

"A week in a hotel in a Spanish city is a grown-up holiday!" said Nan. "*I* will look after the girls!"

Lulu and Mellie had sighed with relief. Nan and Mellie came to stay at Lulu's house so that Lulu's very large collection of animals did not have to be moved anywhere.

That was kind of Nan, because she really

was not an animal sort
of person. Small creatures,
like hamsters, made
her squeal. Larger ones,
like rabbits, that looked
so cuddly and yet had
such sharp claws and teeth, made her

nervous. Parrots, thought
Nan, were perfect for
jungles – but definitely
not perfect for living
rooms.

Dogs were dirty
beasts – large, and
smelly and best out of
doors.

That was what
Nan thought, but
all the same she
bravely packed her

bag and moved across town to stay with the girls.

"It will be no trouble," she said.

Now, already, on the very first morning, here was trouble. A bagful of trouble, tied up at the top and snoring on the doorstep.

"Leave that bag alone!" said Nan as she grabbed Lulu.

Nan was little and snappy and quick and kind. She was also a good strong grabber. She hung on to Lulu and she said, "There could be any savage creature in the world in that bag!"

"Oh, Nan!" protested Lulu, while Mellie said fairly, "Not *any*, Nan! Not *any* savage creature! Nothing much bigger than a small crocodile would actually fit. Or a bear cub might, I suppose. Or a bundle of snakes. . ."

"Mellie!" groaned Lulu. "Stop it! Don't!"

"Don't what?"

"Start Nan off," said Lulu, but it was too late. Nan had already started.

"Snakes!" she cried. "Snakes! Don't you touch it, Lulu! Wait till I get help. Whatever it is, this house needs no more animals! This family needs no more animals! *You* need no more animals, as I have said a thousand times."

"A million times," said Lulu, wriggling away from Nan. "At least. There's a cat in that bag."

"There's more than a cat," said Nan. "One cat is not that size. What are people thinking of, to leave such a thing on someone's doorstep? Lulu, come away!"

"Those snores sound like purrs," said Lulu, not coming away.

"Purrs, or growls," said Mellie.

"Growls!" said Nan. "Growls! I shall complain to someone. The police. The wildlife park. The RSPCA. Whoever is responsible for great growling bags on people's doorsteps! I shall telephone them all, right now. Lulu – do not touch a thing! Mellie – watch her!"

"Yes, Nan," said Mellie, but Lulu did not say yes, too. In fact, the moment Nan was gone she turned back to the bag, and began tugging at the knot once again.

"Nan will go mad," said Mellie, watching.

"Poor Nan," said Lulu. "She just doesn't understand about animals.

She likes flowers best. There!"

The knot was undone.

The bag was open.

Whatever was inside woke up.

"*MeeeOW!*" said the inside of the bag, and out jumped the most enormous cat that Lulu and Mellie had ever seen.

A glow-in-the-dark orange cat with eyes like lime-green sweets. Fur like a cloud. Paws like beanbags. A tail like a fat feather duster.

"WOW!" said Lulu and Mellie, and reached out admiring, grabbing hands.

Perhaps the cat thought they wanted to put it back in the bag. It definitely did not want to be grabbed. It leapt away on its beanbag paws, into the street, across fences and gardens. It vanished like an orange rocket fired off into the sky.

At that moment Nan came out again. Neither the police nor the wildlife park nor the RSPCA had been any help at all. They had played her annoying music, and recorded her cross messages on their answering machines, and that was all.

"Useless!" said Nan, who would have liked rescue vans with flashing lights and sirens, and she went back outside feeling grumpy. Then she saw the empty bag on the doorstep, and that made Nan go off like a rocket too.

"Lulu! For goodness' sake!" she exploded. "You opened that bag? You might have been attacked! The minute my back was turned! What a girl! What a granddaughter! Where have you put the creature, anyway? Do you even know what it was?"

"It was a cat," said Lulu, when she at last got a chance to reply.

"A cat? There was more than one cat in that bag! That looked like a bag full of cats! Now Lulu, tell me, where you have put them?"

"It was one cat," said Lulu, "and I haven't put it anywhere. It ran away."

"Like a rocket," added Mellie. "Whoosh, and then gone!"

"Good," said Nan. "Ran away! Good!'

"Bad," said Lulu.

"Listen, Lulu," said Nan, her crossness fizzing away like the last sparks of a firework. "You don't want a cat! You have enough pets, goodness knows. Dogs. Fish. That parrot. Those terrible squeaking things in the shed. . ."

"Guinea pigs," said Lulu.

"Bad enough having all them," said Nan. "But cats? Worst of all! Bringing in dead birds. . . Bringing in dead mice. . . Who would want a cat?"

Charlie, the boy from next door, came along just then, riding his scooter. He heard what Nan said and stopped to look over the fence and say, "We have a cat."

"Yes, Charlie has a cat," agreed Lulu. "A lovely black and white one called Suzy. She doesn't bring in dead mice and things, does she, Charlie?"

"Not dead ones," said Charlie,

cheerfully. "Live ones, though! She's always bringing in live mice. They get under the fridge."

"Your poor mother," exclaimed Nan.

"See, Lulu! What did I tell you?"

"Once," said Charlie, enjoying Nan's horror, "you must remember, Lulu, because it was at my birthday party and you were there and Mellie was too – there was a bang under the fridge and all the electricity went off. Even my Xbox. And it was ages before it was fixed again."

"Terrible, terrible, terrible," moaned Nan.

"Yes," said Charlie. "I'd got two new Xbox games for my birthday and I couldn't play either of them. And there was no light or heat or hot water either. Or toast. For days. And all because the wires had been chewed up by one of Suzy's mice. . ."

Nan shook her head and groaned. Lulu began to wish very much that Charlie would shut up and go away.

". . .or maybe one of Suzy's rats," said Charlie.

Nan shrieked, and Mellie got the giggles, the way she sometimes did. Choking, silent giggles, like inside explosions.

"I wonder if anyone's looking for you, Charlie," said Lulu. "Perhaps you should go and see."

Charlie took no notice of that. He loved making people shriek and giggle.

"Birds are worse than rats and mice," he told Nan. "They can fly, that's why. So they flap round the house smashing things and they go mad at the windows. You should see the mess the pigeon Suzy brought in yesterday made! Poo everywhere!"

"Charlie!" yelled Lulu. "Do you have to go on and on and on and on?"

"I haven't told you the worst yet," said Charlie. "About the great big. . ."

Mellie had a very good idea. She picked up the empty cloth bag that had held the cat, that was still lying on the step, and pulled it over Charlie's head. He stopped speaking in mid-sentence, very surprised.

"Mellie!" said Nan. "Take that bag off Charlie's head at once!"

"It's all right, I like it," said Charlie from inside the bag. "Want to see me ride my scooter up the street with this bag on my head?"

"Yes, please!" said Lulu and Mellie.

"NO!" cried Nan, and took the cat bag off his head before he could try.

"OK," he said, looking disappointed. "I better go anyway because guess where my family are going any minute now? (That's what I came out to tell you before you kept wanting to know about Suzy.) Away to the seaside with my friend Henry's family! In two caravans. My family in one caravan. Henry's family in another caravan. Suzy the cat in her cat carrier. We're almost ready. We've got loads of air freshener and everyone's wellies and the metal detector because of what happened last time. . ."

"Last time," explained Lulu to Mellie and Nan, "Charlie and Henry buried Charlie's mum's bag for buried treasure and the tide came in before they could find where they put it. . ."

"Was it lost for ever?" asked Nan, horrified.

"Yes," said Charlie. "And everyone blamed Henry and me! As if it was our fault that the sea has tides!"

"One of the things that was lost for ever was the key to their house!" said Lulu. "We had to help them break in when they got back home."

"We had to break into the caravan too," said Charlie, remembering. "That was even worse because Suzy had been shut in for hours and hours. . . Gosh! Pooh! It was awful! We had to sleep with all the windows open and Suzy got out and went beach combing and came back with a stinky dead crab. That's why we've packed all the air freshener. . ."

"Uh!" groaned Nan, and went back into the house so that she did not have to listen to any more Suzy stories.

A few minutes later, Charlie (with the bag on his head again) was loaded into a car and driven away. Then Lulu and Mellie were left alone on the doorstep,

with nothing
to show
that their
mysterious,
snoring
surprise had
ever existed.

"Not even
the bag," said
Mellie sadly.

"Let's go and look for it!" suggested
Lulu.

"Charlie's taken it. Didn't you see?"

"Not the bag! The cat!"

But Nan was not pleased with this
idea. "Who in the world would want a
cat after hearing Charlie?" she demanded.
"Anyway, it is not possible to go cat
hunting just now because . . . because. . ."

Nan searched her brain for a very good

reason not to go cat hunting.

"Because I am taking you out for lunch!" she announced at last. "We will walk through the park, and then have pizzas and afterwards we will go visiting."

Mellie looked at Lulu to see if she minded doing these things instead of cat hunting. Lulu did not mind a bit. She planned to cat hunt all the way to the park, and all through the park and, after lunch, all the time they were visiting friends.

"How lucky I am to have two beautiful granddaughters to take out to lunch!" continued Nan. "Now then, hurry up! Hands, faces, clean teeth, hair, and for goodness' sake, find some tidier clothes!"

"I thought you said we were beautiful," objected Mellie.

"Beautiful? Yes!" said Nan. "Respectable?

No! Lulu! What are you doing with that wheelbarrow?"

Lulu explained that she needed the wheelbarrow to hold the pet carrier. And that she needed the pet carrier in case they should be lucky enough to find the runaway cat from the bag. Because if they did, she would catch that cat and put it in the pet carrier and load it on to the wheelbarrow and take it home.

"And that would be perfect!" said Lulu.

Nan did not think it would be perfect, and she was not very pleased about having to take a wheelbarrow out to lunch. It was rather a nuisance in Pizza Hut.

After lunch, however, Nan agreed that it was a good thing they had brought it along. Then they went visiting a whole collection of Nan's friends. Nan's friends all grew flowers (like Nan did) and detested cats (like Nan did) and thought Lulu and Mellie were wonderful (like Nan did) and gave them strange and useless presents which surprised them so much they kept forgetting to say thank you.

Lulu and Mellie took it in turns to push the wheelbarrow home. Now, as well as the the pet carrier the wheelbarrow held:

A large knitted patchwork blanket.

A rather old teddy bear wearing pirate clothes.

A ship in a bottle that needed glueing.

A very fresh lemon cake on a plate, still hot from the oven and with yellow icing dripping off the top like lava from a volcano.

And an enormous bunch of leftover lilies from the friend who kept the flower shop.

"Atchoo!" sneezed Lulu, the moment she saw them, and she continued to sneeze all the way home, and so did Mellie.

"Did you say thank you for those lilies?" demanded Nan.

Mellie and Lulu shook their heads and sneezed four more times each and bumped the wheelbarrow with each sneeze.

"It's nice to say 'thank you' when someone gives you a present," said Nan. "Even for something you might not want. . . Let me carry those flowers! They are going to slide into the lemon cake any moment!"

Lulu handed the lilies over and Nan began sneezing. She sneezed until she got home, where she thankfully arranged them in a very nice bucket at the end of the garden.

"What are we going to do with the cake?" asked Mellie, lifting it out of the wheelbarrow. It was not as fresh looking at it had been at the beginning of the journey. It was slightly bumped from the ship in the bottle, and slightly stabbed from the pirate bear's sword, and slightly woolly from the blanket, and slightly pollen-dusted from the lilies. It looked more than ever like a volcano.

Nan looked at it thoughtfully.

"Waste not, want not," she said at last. "I'm sure we will enjoy it. Omelettes for supper first. Cake for afterwards. And by the way, I didn't hear, but I hope you both said thank you!"

They hadn't and they knew it. They had been so astonished at being handed a miniature volcano that they hadn't said anything at all, except "Oh!"

"Really!" said Nan. "What terrible manners!"

"I expect we *looked* pleased," said Mellie, hopefully.

"Let us hope so," said Nan, picking up the cake. "Now, then! One of you come and help me cook supper. The other, unpack this wheelbarrow and put everything away!"

"You go with Nan," Lulu told Mellie, as Nan hurried indoors. "I'll put the things away, and then I'm coming out again to look for that cat."

"I'd almost forgotten it," said Mellie.

"I hadn't," said Lulu, who all through the day, at every glimpse of orange (flower or leaf or fur or woolly square in a knitted blanket), had remembered the cat that jumped out of the bag. Where could she begin to hunt for it now, she wondered, as she climbed the stairs with her arms full of presents.

Then she pushed open her bedroom door and found she did not have to hunt at all.

Because there it was.

Wonderful.

Curled up in the middle of her bed.

Snoring.

A gigantic orange heap of fluff.

The cat from the bag!

Beside the cat, a flower, orange, like the cat.

"A marigold," murmured Lulu, who had learned the names of flowers long ago from Nan. "A marigold, and a marigold cat! Perfect!"

Chapter Two

The Cat in the Night

The marigold cat had been asleep when Lulu came in, but now its eyes were half open, gazing at Lulu.

"Now what?" they seemed to ask. "It has been a bad day. Thrown out of my home. The time in that bag. No food. No peace. Nowhere to rest (until I found your window open). Now what?"

Lulu understood. She had always found it easy to think the way an animal does. She could guess that although the cat on her bed looked as soft and relaxed as a cuddly toy, underneath its fluff it was wondering: *Need I jump out of the window? Or not?*

That was why she did not rush to stroke or cuddle the marigold cat. Instead, she tried to make it feel as if lying on her bed was a safe and normal thing to do.

"Don't worry," she murmured to the cat as she began arranging the presents. "Don't jump. Don't bother about me at all."

Mellie had brought a chair to sleep
on that unfolded at night into a little
bed. The cat watched as Lulu spread the

patchwork
quilt over it.
It yawned
when she
sat the pirate
bear on the
window sill.
It blinked

while she uncorked the ship in the bottle
and peered thoughtfully inside.

When Nan called "Supper", Lulu left

everything
where it was,
the blanket on
the chair, the
bear on the
window sill,

the ship in the bottle, and the marigold cat curled on the bed.

I don't need to jump out of the window, thought the cat thankfully.

There was always a lot to do at the end of a day in Lulu's house. The ancient parrot liked to be scratched and talked to while he watched his favourite cooking programme. The guinea pigs needed fresh hay and carrots. The old dog, Sam, had to be given his old dog medicine. The young dog, Rocko, had to be worn out with wild chases up and down the little garden. Last of all the rabbits had to be taken from their runs and put to bed. The boy rabbits in the boy rabbit hutch. The girl rabbits in the girl rabbit hutch.

Nan and Mellie helped with all these jobs. Nan measured out medicine and

Mellie threw balls for Rocko. Nan found
the right TV channel for the parrot.
Mellie washed
the guinea pigs'
carrots. Nan was
very strict with
the rabbits.

Lulu did the
rabbit catching,
the hay cleaning,
the poo removing
and the parrot
scratching. All the time that everyone was
working, Nan talked about how many

pets Lulu had, compared to the number
Nan thought it would be sensible to have.

"Guinea pigs!" she said to Lulu. "Now
Lulu, that is very interesting. Guinea pigs
are not meant to be pets at all. . . No! In
South America, did you know they are
eaten as food? That's what guinea pigs
are *meant* for! Not keeping as pets in an
English shed!"

"Nan!" exclaimed Mellie. "Would you
really like to eat Socks and Mittens?"

Nan said of course not. What a

suggestion! Terrible! She was only explaining why guinea pigs were such very bad pets. And also she wondered if Lulu had ever thought that it might be a good idea to give both the guinea pigs and the rabbits to the pet farm in town, where Lulu could visit them whenever she liked.

"And then there would be none of this cleaning out," explained Nan. "Or sawdust, or smells, or worrying every night if all the rabbits are where they should be. . ."

"You don't have to worry," said Lulu. "One little mix-up wouldn't really matter."

"Oh yes it would, Lulu!" said Nan. "Oh yes it would! And another thing! About the dogs. . ."

The dogs, who had been listening, now pricked up their ears. They always knew when they were being talked about. They also knew how much they bothered Nan. They always had. Every time one of them ate a letter, or licked out a bowl on the table, or sat down suddenly just where she was walking, or fell asleep in a doorway, or rolled muddily on the sofa, she got cross. The fuss she made when they did their mad barking at the visitors was awful. *Nan*, thought the dogs, *fussed about everything*. Play-fighting in the kitchen. Eating soap in the bathroom. Bones in the living room. She thought they were bad dogs.

"The pet farm doesn't have dogs," remarked Lulu, cheerfully. Nan's plans to get rid of her animals did not worry her at all. Lulu was used to them. Nan thought of new ones every time she visited.

"Very sensible of the pet farm," said

Nan. "But listen, Lulu! I have a very kind friend who would be glad to have an old dog like Sam for company."

"But would they like Rocko too?" asked Lulu, wickedly.

"It would be unkind to split them up," agreed Mellie.

"Rocko, no," admitted Nan, looking in disgust at Rocko, who was chomping a mouthful of guinea-pig food, swallowing the bits he liked and letting the rest dribble all green and slimy from the corners of his mouth.

"I cannot think of anyone who would be glad to have Rocko," admitted Nan. "Not as he is! But I am sure there are dog training classes that he could go to. I have seen them on television, absolutely dreadful dogs, nearly as bad as him, taught to sit and walk. . ."

At the word "walk", Rocko flung himself with delight at Nan, and tried to kiss her with green slime kisses. Lulu grabbed him just in time, while Mellie began her exploding giggles again.

"Lulu," ordered Nan, "before you do anything else, please wash that dog's face!"

Lulu washed Rocko's face with goldfish water.

"You haven't thought of a way of getting rid of the goldfish yet," Mellie reminded Nan.

"The fish are easy," said Nan. "The pond in the park is full of fish. A few more would do no harm."

"And the parrot?"

"I'm sure he could go to the pet farm with the rabbits," said Nan. "It would be a nice change for him. All he does is sit on top of that cage all day."

"He likes sitting on top of his cage," pointed out Lulu. "He could sit anywhere else if he wanted. He doesn't like change. He's very old."

"How old?"

"More than eighty," said Lulu.

"Good gracious heavens!" cried Nan. "Then he should be in a museum! At least let us thank goodness that bag full of cats disappeared. Cats are the worst!"

"What, worse than Rocko?" asked Mellie, and her giggles, which had never really left her all afternoon, began again.

"You heard what Charlie said about the cat they have next door! How sorry I am for that boy's mother!"

"Lots of people are sorry for Charlie's mother," remarked Lulu. "But not because of his cat!"

"Well, well," said Nan. "Charlie is in

his caravan and the animals are put away for the night! We can forget them for a while. Come along in now! It's been a long, long day. Who'll fetch my bag from my room?"

Mellie was the nearest to the foot of the stairs, and she was halfway up before Lulu could begin to rush after her.

"Not in your *shoes*, Lulu!" exclaimed Nan, stopping her at as she passed. "And I didn't see you wash your hands either! Back into the kitchen, please!"

Lulu kicked off her shoes, scrubbed her hands at the kitchen sink, and waited in agony for Mellie to appear and announce, "You'll never guess what I've just found upstairs!"

It didn't happen. Mellie seemed to be gone for a very long time, but she returned with the bag and handed it to

Nan without a word about marigold cats. Lulu looked at her anxiously. Had she seen, or hadn't she? Perhaps she had just gone into

Nan's room. Perhaps the cat had changed its mind, and jumped out of the window after all. Perhaps. . .

"That patchwork blanket looks very nice on my chair," said Mellie, sweetly, ignoring Lulu's glares.

"I hope you said thank you for it," remarked Nan, a little vaguely. "Come with me now, Lulu, and see what I am making."

Nan did not do knitting, as many grandmothers do. She made things with beads strung on thin silver threads. She got out her beads and wires from her bag,

and showed Lulu the necklace she was
making, a rainbow loop of flowers. "Very
nearly finished," she said. "Then I will
have two. One for you. . ." Nan yawned
a tiny, ladylike yawn ". . .one for Mellie.
Hmmm, hmmm," said Nan sleepily, and
closed her eyes.

Lulu, who had been holding the
flowery necklace to admire it, laid it very,
very gently on Nan's knee.

Nan did not move.

Silently, Lulu stood up.

Across the room, and just as silently,
Mellie did the same.

Nan gave a very small snore.

Lulu's eyes met Mellie's. Mellie, Lulu
could see, was about to explode. Nan
snored again, and Lulu shot across the
room, grabbed Mellie and dragged her to
the kitchen.

"Oh! Oh! Oh!" gasped Mellie, bent over and shaking. "Two snores! Lulu, that cat's asleep on your bed, did you know?"

Lulu nodded.

"What'll we do?"

"Feed it," said Lulu. "Quickly, before Nan wakes up. Oh, Mellie, please don't snort! Help me instead!"

She began to load a tray. Tuna fish. Water. Milk. Cheese crackers. Cold ham. Mellie recovered in time to add a leftover omelette. They carried it upstairs and pushed open the bedroom door. The marigold cat looked up worriedly, measuring the distance between itself and the window. "Look!" whispered Lulu, and lowered the tray, and the cat looked and began to purr like an engine.

Just as the marigold cat was the largest cat by far that Lulu and Mellie had ever

seen, so the marigold cat's purring was
the loudest they had ever heard.

It purred as they stroked it. It purred
as it chewed up everything on the tray.
It purred even when wrapped in the
patchwork quilt. It purred by itself alone
in the bedroom when they took away the
supper tray and crept back downstairs to
wash the empty plates. They could hear it
in the kitchen, and they could hear it in
the living room, and in her dreams, Nan
heard it too.

"Was I snoring?" she asked, waking up with a jump. "Lulu, I dreamed I heard myself snoring! It can't be true! I never have! Snoring! Was I? Now, Mellie, tell me the truth!"

Mellie became speechless and had to lie on the floor.

"Lulu?" asked Nan, pleadingly.

"You were snoring a little tiny bit, but hardly anything at all," Lulu told her truthfully.

Nan looked as horrified as if Lulu had said, "Your head was falling off a little tiny bit, but hardly anything at all."

So Lulu added kindly, "But I don't think that's what you heard. . ."

Lulu paused. There was no sound from upstairs any more. No purring. Nothing. And anyway, what could she say? "I think you heard the marigold cat?" Certainly not!

"Perhaps a helicopter flew over," she suggested to Nan. "Maybe you heard that. Or a motorbike, revving up. A lawnmower, even. . ."

"Helicopters!" wailed poor Nan, who up until the last few minutes had believed she spent all her sleep hours in ladylike silence. "Motorbikes! Lawnmowers! I sounded like that! Tomorrow I shall go to the doctor!"

"For snoring?" asked Mellie, rolling around on the carpet, and she laughed so much that Lulu could not help joining in too.

Suddenly, in the middle of the laughter, and the middle of Nan's wailing, came a sound that startled them all into silence.

Heavy feet. Beanbag feet. Treading hard and loud, creaking the floorboards of the room overhead.

Sam and Rocko, who had been dozing by the fire, woke and put back their ears and growled. All down the middle of their backs a line of fur stood up like grass.

"Whatever is that?" whispered Nan.

Lulu and Mellie knew what it was, of course: the marigold cat. What else could it be?

"A ghost?" asked Lulu hopefully.

The dogs began to bark.

Nan was on her feet. She did not believe in ghosts. She believed in burglars. She was not afraid of them, though. She was not afraid of anything (except being heard to snore). Brave as a lion, she rolled her magazine into a weapon, ordered, "Girls – stay here with the dogs! Dogs – guard the girls!" and charged up the stairs.

Lulu and Mellie charged after her.

The dogs did not. They dared not. They knew who was the boss. Nan. "Dogs Downstairs" was the absolute rule when Nan was visiting. Not even the smell of the most enormous marigold cat in the world could entice them to break it. They stayed at the foot of the stairs whimpering and yowling while Lulu, Mellie and Nan hunted through the two bedrooms and the bathroom and the airing cupboard.

And found nothing but flowers. Two flowers. A marigold on Lulu's bed. A blue flower like a star, caught on the window sill.

"Love-in-a-mist," said Nan, closing the window. "Lulu? Mellie?"

"Mmm?" they said.

"Is there something perhaps you are not telling me?"

Lulu and Mellie nodded.

"Something bad?"

"No, no! Very nice."

"About these flowers?"

"Yes, very nice about the flowers," agreed Lulu, and all at once began yawning and yawning. Mellie caught Lulu's yawns, just as Lulu had caught Mellie's giggles, and suddenly they could not stop.

"Bed," said Nan. "And sleep. And sweet dreams. No ghosts! What a silly idea!"

"Yes," agreed Lulu.

"Burglars are impossible. With two dogs downstairs. . ." She glared down the stairs at the dogs, who rolled on their backs to show they understood.

". . .and me upstairs in the room next door. What could be safer?"

"Nothing," said Lulu and Mellie, hugging her.

They went to bed, with their windows closed and their bedroom doors open, so that Nan could rush to the rescue at the slightest sound. With her magazine.

"Not that I shall need to," said Nan.

The house became dark. And quiet (except for the gentle sound of helicopter snoring). Mellie on her chair bed snuffled with giggles in her sleep. The dogs ran in dreams, with silent, twitching feet. Only Lulu was awake.

Very quietly, Lulu crept out of bed and opened her bedroom window again. And soon afterwards the beanbag paws began creaking the floorboards, just like before.

"Lovely, lovely marigold cat," murmured

Lulu, more asleep than awake, and then completely asleep.

After that neither Lulu nor Nan nor Mellie heard a single sound all night.

Daisies, cat mint, and feathery grasses. Poppies. More marigolds. More love-in-a-mist. Flowers on the landing. Flowers on Nan's bedside rug. Flowers on the bath mat.

But most of all on Lulu's bed, where the marigold cat, tired out with all its hunting and collecting, curled up into a huge, orange, snoring, purring heap of fur.

And was discovered by Nan in the morning.

Chapter Three

The Cat and the Dogs

"Well!" said Nan, indignantly, gazing at her sleeping granddaughters, and the sleeping, snoring marigold cat. "Well!"

And she went and fetched her magazine and rolled it up again.

She used it to prod, very gently, the marigold cat.

The marigold cat gave one last snore and opened its eyes and blinked at Nan. It smiled a curly, cat-shaped smile. It seemed to understand that Nan was no danger. Then it stretched and jumped from Lulu's bed, and landed with a thump and a burglarish creak of floorboards beside Nan.

Lulu woke first.

Very slowly.

Pushing her face in her pillow.

Yawning.

Remembering.

Stretching out a hand for the marigold cat.

"Are you still there?" she asked sleepily. "What were you doing all night, in and out of the window? Are those more flowers? Oh!"

"Yes, oh!" said Nan sternly.

"Hello Nan!"

"Hello Lulu."

"Look at all the flowers."

"I am looking at the flowers," said Nan.

"And at the other thing. This orange,
snoring thing! (Didn't I tell you, Lulu,
that I never snored!) This jumped-out-
the-bag-and-ran-away thing! Run away
again!" Nan told the marigold cat.

The marigold cat hooked up a stem of
love-in-the-mist with its beanbag paw, and
laid it at Nan's feet like a present.

"It likes you," said Lulu, and Mellie rolled over and said sleepily, "Course it does."

The marigold cat stayed to breakfast. Scrambled eggs. Dog biscuits, Weetabix and milk, all cooked and served by Nan.

"I have never starved anyone yet," said Nan. "And I am not about to begin now. But Lulu, you cannot keep that animal! Just listen to those dogs!"

The dogs had to be shut outside while the marigold cat ate breakfast. They were outraged. The old dog Sam squashed his nose into the crack under the door and bayed. The young dog Rocko leapt up and down outside the kitchen window. Every time he popped up he woofed one very loud, shocked woof. Every time he vanished he growled.

The noise was so much that nobody heard the postman knocking outside. So he pushed the door open instead, and began to announce, "Your dogs are going mad out here," but the last two words were said from flat on the floor, as he was knocked down by Sam and Rocko, charging in to confront the marigold cat. They ran in a straight line. Over the postman. Over chairs. Barging under the table, shaking off the plates. Mellie

shouted. Lulu dived to grab their collars.
Nan waved her magazine over her head.
The marigold cat swelled to an enormous
size.

Biff! went a beanbag paw. Once on
Rocko's nose. Once on Sam's.

"WOW!" yowled the dogs, and turned
and ran, back the way they had come,
knocking down more chairs, more plates
and Mellie as they passed. The postman
was trampled again. Nan and the marigold
cat remained standing.

After that the dogs were miserable.
They lay on the grass and held their
noses and cried. Even when Lulu lured
them in with biscuits they were not
happy. They crawled past the marigold
cat, shivering. The marigold cat sat on the
bottom stair and washed her biffing paw
thoughtfully when they passed.

The dogs stopped wanting to go upstairs. They stopped trying to lick plates on the table. They stopped falling asleep in inconvenient places. They got in their baskets without being told. In their baskets they yowled and growled, non-stop. Nothing anyone could do would comfort them.

"Nan's right," said Mellie. "The marigold cat can't stay here. It's not fair to the poor dogs."

Lulu knew that was true. The dogs had

no peace, and neither did the marigold cat. It was trying to make a flower collection, but wherever it went with its flowers, there was fuss.

In the living room was the parrot. He sat safe out of biffing range on the top of his cage and shrieked and flapped at the poor marigold cat.

It was not peaceful in the kitchen either, with the dogs in their baskets, yowling and growling and holding their noses. And where the dogs did not go, Nan went.

"Not in there

please, your majesty!" she said, when the marigold cat, looking for a little quiet, curled up in a marigold heap in the airing cupboard.

"Out you come!" she ordered, when the marigold cat began a daisy collection under Lulu's bed.

Nan divided the marigold cat's flower collection between the vases and the compost heap, depending on how healthy the flowers looked.

"What kind of cat are you?" she said to the cat. "Terrifying the dogs! Scaring the bird! Gathering flowers! What kind of a cat is that? If you *are* a cat!"

It was Mellie who noticed that when they went shopping Nan bought a packet of salmon-flavoured cat treats and hid them in her bag.

"Nan," said Lulu hopefully. "The dogs don't like the marigold cat. But I think you do."

"Is that what you think?" asked Nan.

"Yes I do," said Lulu, "and so does Mellie. And we have been wondering if when you go home the marigold cat could go too, to live with you."

"Is that what you've been wondering?"

"Yes," said Lulu.

"Yes," said Mellie.

"Just because you like something doesn't mean you want it to come and live with you," protested Nan. "For instance, I like your friend Charlie, but I wouldn't want him to come and live with me. . ."

"Charlie is different," said Lulu.

"He's bonkers," said Mellie.

"It's not fair to compare the marigold cat to Charlie," said Lulu. "They are not a bit alike."

The marigold cat, who had been listening to the conversation, blinked in agreement.

"Well then, not Charlie," said Nan. "Someone else! The Queen! I like her too, but I also wouldn't want her to come and live with me. (Although I wouldn't mind a short visit.)"

"How short?" interrupted Mellie.

"Three or four days. But as for that marigold-enormous-cat, it is just not my problem! *You* should not have let it out of the bag."

"Nan!" said Lulu reproachfully.

"I am not a cat person. I am a garden person."

"The marigold cat is a garden cat," said Mellie, and as if to prove it, the marigold cat went out and found a new flower for Nan from the front flower bed.

"Hmmm," said Nan. "Chickweed. Flowers from the garden of every house in the street. Weeds from here."

"We tried planting flowers," said Lulu. "But the dogs dug them up as fast as we planted them. They're no good at gardening. They don't understand. But I'm sure the marigold cat would be different."

"I'm sure the marigold cat would be the same," said Nan.

Lulu did not argue any more. She went to the shed and fetched a garden spade. Mellie went with her, and collected a garden fork.

"What about those silly dogs?"
asked Nan.

The marigold cat sat down by the
flower bed and cleaned its biffing
paw.

That day, in between zookeeping and
dog walking and cat food shopping, Lulu
and Mellie dug the flower bed.

The next morning they went with Nan
to the market for plants. In the middle
of the flower bed they planted a little
green bush. All round the edge, a circle
of pansies – bright colours like the beads
Nan wove into necklaces.

Rocko and Sam could hardly bear it.
They longed to garden as well. They
longed to scoop out dog-shaped hollows
and roll in the dust. They longed to dig
for interesting bones. They longed to
scrabble large holes, like rabbit traps.

They longed to scratch up the pansies and gnaw the roots of the little green bush. That was the dogs' sort of gardening.

It was not the cat's sort of gardening, and it would not allow it.

It sat on guard under the little green bush, and when any dogs came by it got ready its biffing paw. It biffed Sam when he

arrived with his smelly old bone, looking for somewhere to plant a smelly-old-bone tree. When Rocko sneaked past and grabbed a pansy, the marigold cat chased him all across the garden.

"Perhaps you are a garden cat," said

Nan, getting
out her cat
treats.

The dogs
gave up
trying to do
gardening
and went to

sulk in their baskets instead. They glared
at the marigold cat from between
their paws, as if they were thinking of
vanishing magic.

Perhaps they were thinking of vanishing
magic.

The very day after the flower bed was
planted, the marigold cat disappeared.

Chapter Four

The Cat and the Flowers

One day the marigold cat was there, eating enormous meals three times a day, organizing the dogs, bringing in flowers, curling up in dark places from which it was chased.

The next it was gone.

It was nowhere in the house. The dogs proved that. They came joyfully out of their baskets and began making up for lost time, grabbing things off the table, sleeping in doorways, chewing up the post as it came through the letter box.

Nan telephoned the police. The RSPCA. The wildlife park people. All her friends. Everyone she could think of who might know how to find a cat.

No one was any use.

Then Lulu and Mellie and Nan were very sad. They imagined all the terrible things that might have happened to the marigold cat.

Starving.

Run over.

Kidnapped.

Back (poor thing) in a bag.

To cheer them up, Nan's friends came to visit and to say how sorry they were to hear that the wonderful animal, about whom Nan had told them so many good things, had suddenly vanished. They were all very kind, and they all brought presents for Lulu and Mellie. The presents (half a bottle of lavender perfume, a woolly hat, a CD of Christmas carols played on a trumpet, and a book about jungles without any pictures) were so surprising that Lulu and Mellie had to be reminded to say thank you nearly every time. Instead of what they usually said, which was, "What! Is that for me? Goodness!"

"It is good manners," Nan reminded them, "to say thank you when someone gives you a present."

"Yes, Nan," said Lulu and Mellie.

Each time one of Nan's friends visited, Nan told the story of the marigold cat again. How she had at last found a perfect pet. A flower loving, dog controlling, perfect pet. Each time the story got a little bit sadder.

The dogs were not sorry the marigold cat had gone. They were very glad. You could tell by the way they swaggered through the house, their eyes three-corner twinkling gleams, their tails like flags of victory.

"You needn't be so pleased," said Lulu, crossly. "Because I am going to find that marigold cat! And you," she added, suddenly inspired, "are going to help!"

The dogs fell about laughing with their tongues hanging out.

"Never, never, never!" they seemed to say.

"Oh yes you are," said Lulu, and clipped on their leads.

"How Lulu?" demanded Mellie. "How could they possibly help?"

"The police use dogs for tracking," said Nan, looking almost a little bit hopeful.

"*Brainy* dogs, though," said Mellie, and Nan stopped looking hopeful. Rocko's lead was already tangled round his unbrainy legs. Sam had forgotten he was wearing one, and was trying to walk under the fence.

"They're not very brainy," admitted Lulu, untangling Rocko and hauling back Sam, "but I think they might be brainy enough."

They started in the garden. They had searched it before, but not with the dogs. Lulu watched them closely as she led them around. By the edge of the fence. In and out of the guinea-pig shed. Nowhere near the flower bed. (The dogs no longer cared for gardening. The biffing monster had seen to that.) All along the

rabbit hutches, though, and under the
bushes.

The dogs remained as cheerful as ever.
"They wouldn't look like that if the
marigold cat was hiding in the garden,"
said Lulu. "We'd better try the street."

Nan waited at the gate while she and
Mellie set off together.

"Down to the end one way," said Lulu,

"and then back, and past the gate, and down to the other end. And then we'll cross over. Come on!"

It was a sunny, friendly evening. Lots of neighbours were out in their gardens. "Do you mind," asked Lulu and Mellie, "if we come and look for a cat?"

No one minded, and so Lulu and Mellie and the happy-tailed dogs looked at gardens with poppies, love-in-a-mist and daisies. Gardens with roses and long tickling grasses. Gardens with weeds and gardens with vegetables.

They went all the way to the end of the street and back to Nan at the gate without a hint of the marigold cat.

"Now we'll try the other way," said Lulu.

The dogs looked less cheerful. Rocko had been hoping that now they would go to the park. Sam thought it was high time they went home and did a bit more annoying of Nan.

"The other way," insisted Lulu, tugging their leads.

The other way was not so interesting. They raced past Charlie's house, and the one next door to it that was as neat as a painted picture. They went right to the corner where Henry lived. "That's far enough!" called Nan from the gate, so they turned again, the dogs now very bouncy because their noses were pointing towards home, Lulu and Mellie walking slowly, inspecting the flowers in every garden.

"Marigolds in Charlie's," said Lulu. "I didn't notice before."

They paused to look. Charlie's house seemed half asleep with no family home, and no Suzy on the window sill.

The dogs did not want to stop at Charlie's house. They tried to pull Lulu and Mellie past. Their eyes were no longer three-cornered gleams of mischief. Their tails no longer waved like flags.

"Aha!" said Lulu, and opened the garden gate.

The dogs sat down, and looked mutinous.

"Let's go round the back," said Lulu. "No one would mind. They'd know we're not burglars. Come on, Mellie! Come on, dogs!"

Very, very grumpily the dogs slouched after Lulu and Mellie.

Along the little path.

Round past the picnic table.

Into the back garden.

It was extremely quiet.

No Charlie. No Charlie's family. No Suzy. No birds on the empty bird table. No sign of life. . .

Except. . .

One wilted marigold, caught in the cat flap.

Down on her stomach went Lulu, peering through the cat flap.

"Worra, worra, worra," moaned the dogs in despair, and they pulled on their leads to pull Lulu away.

But Lulu saw.

The marigold cat had found a peaceful place for its flower collection at last. A trail of flowers led across the kitchen floor. There was a whole heap in the corner by Charlie's wellington boots. And on top of the heap, like an indoor bonfire, curled up and snoring (or maybe purring) slept the marigold cat.

"Nan! Nan! Nan!" screamed Mellie, dashing back into the street with the dogs behind her. "We've found it! We've found it, on a heap of flowers in Charlie's kitchen! Lulu's there now, watching through the cat flap!"

"Good gracious heavens!" cried Nan. "What a wonderful thing!"

"Come and help us break down the door!"

But it was not necessary to break down the door. Because ever since Charlie had buried his mother's bag for buried treasure and the family had returned from holiday to find themselves locked out, a spare key had been left at Lulu's house, just in case. And while Lulu watched through the cat flap and Rocko and Sam moaned in despair, Mellie and Nan hunted out that key and opened the door.

And then they stared and stared and stared and stared.

And the marigold cat opened her eyes and purred and purred and purred and purred.

"I shall have to sit down," said Nan,

and she did, at Charlie's mum's kitchen table, with her head in her hands.

The marigold cat looked at Nan from amongst its orange cloud of fur, blinking its lime-green eyes, swishing its feather-duster tail. Then, very slowly, on beanbag paws, it padded across to Nan.

The marigold cat was carrying something yellow, which she laid at Nan's feet.

A marigold kitten.

And while Nan was saying, "Oh! What! Oh! Oh my goodness!" she fetched another.

Two marigold kittens.

Nan's swallowed and mopped her eyes and her mouth opened and closed, but she did not say a word.

"Nan," said Lulu, while Mellie exploded in a heap of giggles, "if someone gives you a present, it's nice to say thank you!"

When Nan went back to her own house
the cats went too, and the first thing she

did when she got there was invite all her friends round to admire them.

At Lulu's house, Rocko and Sam crawled out of their baskets and sighed with relief.

"We called them Dandelion and Daisy," Lulu told Charlie when he returned from holiday. "Dandy and Daisy. Perfect names. And perfect pets for Nan. They can help in the garden, and look after the dogs when I take them to visit, and whenever she snores she can say it's the cats."

"Does she snore?" asked Charlie.

"She says not," replied Lulu.

"And is she still mad that you and Mellie opened that bag?"

"Not at all," said Lulu. "She's very pleased! She said 'Thank you!' That's what she said. 'Thank you, thank you, thank you!' And she said, over and over, 'I knew there was more than one cat in that bag.'"

Look out for more

Lulu

adventures.

Lulu
and the Duck in the Park

Hilary McKay

Lulu
and the Dog from the Sea

Hilary McKay

Have you read Hilary McKay's

Charlie
books?

Meet Charlie – he's trouble!